DISCARD

Snow White
A
Hidden Picture
Fairy Tale

From The Brothers Grimm

Oregon Trail Elementary
Media Center

Retold and Illustrated by
Kit Wray

BELL
BOOKS

3265000042337

To Arlynn, Beth, and John

Copyright © 1991 by Boyds Mills Press
All rights reserved
Published by Bell Books
Boyds Mills Press, Inc.
A Highlights Company
910 Church Street
Honesdale, Pennsylvania 18431

Publisher Cataloging-in-Publication Data

Wray, Kit.
  Snow White: A hidden picture fairy tale / retold and illustrated by Kit Wray.
  32 p. : ill. ; cm. (A Hidden picture fairy tale)
Summary: The classic tale of a princess disowned by her stepmother and
protected by seven dwarves until she is rescued by a prince. Illustrations
border the text and include hidden pictures.
ISBN 1-878093-26-6
1. Fairy tales—Juvenile Literature. 2. Folklore—Germany—Juvenile Literature.
3. Literary recreations—Juvenile Literature. [1. Fairy tales. 2. Folklore—
Germany. 3. Literary recreations.] I. Grimm, Jacob,
1785-1863. II. Grimm, Wilhelm, 1786-1859. III. Title. IV. Series.
398.2/2/0943-dc20   [E]   1991
LC Card Number 90-85902
Distributed by St. Martin's Press
Printed in the United States of America

Long ago a queen sat by her window sewing. As she gazed out at the gently falling snow, she happened to prick her finger with a needle. The queen thought to herself, "Would that I had a child as white as snow, as red as blood, and as black as this ebony window frame."

At last a baby girl was born to her with skin as white as snow, lips red as blood, and hair like the blackest ebony. She named the child Snow White.

But while the child was yet an infant, the queen died.

bird, rat, crane, man's face, heads of eagle, dog, pig   1

In time the king took another wife who was beautiful but terribly proud. High in the castle tower she kept a magic looking glass. The queen would often stand before the glass and ask . . .

squirrel, crow, face, elephant, candle, heads of lion, horse, cat, rabbit

"Mirror, mirror on the wall, who is fairest of us all?"
And the looking glass would reply,
"Thou, O Queen, art the fairest of all."
Then she was content, because the mirror always spoke truthfully.

As years passed, the princess Snow White grew into a beautiful girl. Everyone dwelling in the castle loved her dearly, except the queen.

One day when the queen stood before her looking glass, it gave this answer:

"O Queen, the fairest of all is Snow White."

flower, hatchet, brontosaurus, duck, fish, heads of goose, ape, eagle

In her jealous hatred she called a huntsman and said, "Take Snow White to the wilderness. Kill her there and bring me her heart as proof that the girl is dead."

After the huntsman had led Snow White into the forest, he was moved with pity. He released her, saying, "Run quickly, child."

As she disappeared in the shadows, he slew a young fawn and returned to the queen with its heart.

Alone and terrified, Snow White hurried beneath the dark, silent trees. The branches tore her clothing, while small animals darted from her path.

flamingo, lizard, dove, heads of alligator, squirrel

bat, cardinal, pie, snail, duck, woman, face, hunting bow, heads of mouse, cow, deer, elk   7

All that day she never rested in her flight. As the sun sank low in the sky, the exhausted girl came to a clearing in the forest.

There she saw a small cottage. When no one answered her knocking, she opened the door and stepped inside.

sea gull, alligator, banana, weasel, heads of rabbit, walrus, wolf

By the dim light she saw a low table with seven little chairs. She took a bit of food from each place and a small sip from each mug, so nothing would be missed.

Seven small beds were lined up against the wall. Feeling very tired, Snow White lay down upon the last one. Closing her eyes, she quickly fell into a deep sleep.

shovel, sickle, fork, elf's hat, hippopotamus's head, sea horse   9

As the moon floated over the surrounding hills, seven dwarves returned from their work in the mines. But after entering the cottage they soon discovered that someone had been eating at their table.

lobster, quail, seal, cat, heads of hamster, fox, hawk

They searched the cottage and finally found Snow White curled up fast asleep. "What a beautiful child!" they exclaimed, as they gathered round to see. But they were careful not to disturb her.

When Snow White awoke the next morning, she was frightened, but the dwarves kindly asked her name and how she had come there.

"I am called Snow White," she replied. She told of her stepmother's plan to kill her, and of her flight through the forest.

"You may dwell here safe from harm," said one, "if you will cook and keep the house clean." Snow White felt safe with the little men and happily agreed.

"Every morning we leave for the mountains and delve all day for copper and gold." But they warned her, "Let no one in while we are away."

axe, oar, pear, witch's hat, bird, heads of seal, vulture

crescent moon, bread, crown, face, shark, heads of parrot, mole   13

That night the queen came again to her looking glass, thinking that Snow White was dead.

"Mirror, mirror on the wall, who is fairest of us all?"

But the glass gave this answer,

"O Queen, your beauty is fair to behold, but Snow White is still fairer a thousandfold."

The huntsman had betrayed her! Now she peered into the glass and saw Snow White safe with the seven dwarves.

The queen pondered what to do while her anger mounted. At last she dressed herself as a peddler woman and journeyed to the mountains to find their cottage.

Knocking at the door, she disguised her voice. "Fine wares to sell," she said.
Snow White looked out and saw only an old peddler.

parrot, fish, goat, dwarf's face, heads of wolf, dragon   15

"Laces of every color," said the woman as she held one for the girl to see. Snow White saw no harm and unbolted the door.

"Here's a pretty one," said the woman. "Come, and I will lace you with it properly." Then the queen laced her so tightly that Snow White lost her breath and fell senseless.

The queen returned to the castle laughing, "Now I am the fairest!"

girl's face, kangaroo, heads of bird, puppy, shark, rabbit, pig

That evening the seven dwarves found Snow White where she had fallen. Seeing the tight laces that bound her, they quickly cut them away. Soon she began to breathe freely again.

The dwarves now insisted that Snow White should open the door to no one.

Again the queen stood before her looking glass.

"Mirror, mirror on the wall, who is the fairest of us all?"

But the glass still replied, "O Queen, Snow White is yet fairest of all."

"Now I will surely put an end to that girl," cried the queen, and she set out for the cottage dressed as a farmer's wife. This time she carried with her a beautiful comb soaked with poison.

salamander, mushroom, mouse, chickadee, heads of crow, dog

"Fine combs for sale," called a voice from outside the cottage.

"I cannot open to anyone," answered Snow White.

Seeing the delicate comb through the window, she finally stepped out for a closer look. But when the comb was placed in her hair, she sank lifeless into the grass.

18   duck, mouse, snake, bird, heads of camel, lion

As they approached the cottage at sunset, the seven dwarves spied Snow White on the ground. Dropping their tools, they removed the comb from her hair, and the girl soon revived. Again they begged her to remain inside.

starfish, trout, pointing hand, grasshopper, heads of eagle, horse   19

That same night the queen strode up to her looking glass.

"Mirror, mirror on the wall, who is the fairest of us all?"

And it gave the answer, "O Queen, Snow White still lives, and her fair beauty surpasses all."

In her fury the queen vowed she would destroy Snow White. Bearing her candle, she climbed to a quiet, lonely tower of the castle.

dragonfly, drum, heads of dog, pig, gull, ant

There she lit a fire and gathered all her powers to prepare a fatal poison.

When it was ready, she dipped one side of a rosy apple into it. Dressed as a peasant, she again traveled through the wood and knocked at the cottage door. She carried with her a basket of apples, with the poisoned one on top.

Snow White was busy preparing dinner when a voice called from outside, "Sweet apples for sale."

"The dwarves have forbidden me to open the door," called Snow White from the window.

"As you wish," said the woman, "but I'll give you this one."

The woman bit from the apple and offered the other side to Snow White, saying, "It is perfectly good, as you can see."

The apple looked so delicious that Snow White opened the door and reached out for it. As soon as the apple touched her lips, she fell dead to the ground.

mop, dagger, bone, crow, teapot, crab

When the seven dwarves
returned from the hills,
Snow White lay still and
not breathing. They lifted
her up and searched for
anything poisonous, but at
last they saw that their
beloved child was dead. She
looked so fresh and alive
they could not bury her in
the dark ground. So they
made her a coffin out of
clear glass.

frog, carrot, owl, heads of hippopotamus, cow, deer   23

They carried her coffin to a high mountain, and one of them was always there to watch over her, both day and night.

For a long time Snow White lay unchanged, until one spring a king's son passed through the forest. When he saw the glass coffin on the mountain, he was moved by the girl's beauty.

bear, triceratops's head, hamster, seal, scottie dog, brontosaurus

He offered the dwarves anything they might want in exchange for the coffin. At last they gave it to him freely, for it seemed he could not live without being able to see Snow White. Thus, the prince bade his men to carry the coffin away.

As they descended the rocky path, one of the servants stumbled. The poisoned fruit was loosened from Snow White's throat.

"Where am I?" she asked when they had set her down.

"You are here with me," said the prince. "Come to my father's palace to be my wife."

She returned with him happily, and a magnificent wedding was planned.

hawk, beetle, crane, heads of swan, pony, ape

The queen was bidden to the celebration, and wearing her finest robes she asked again,

"Mirror, mirror on the wall, who is fairest of us all?"

And now it gave this answer:

"O Queen, thou art fairest here I hold,

But the new queen is fairer a thousandfold."

The queen could not resist going to see the bride. But when she saw Snow White beside the prince, she stood motionless with terror. Then red-hot iron shoes were brought for her to dance in until she fell dead.

But Snow White lived joyfully with her prince for the rest of her days.

Have You Found Them All?

Long ago a queen sat by her window sewing. As she gazed out at the gently falling snow she happened to prick her finger with a needle. The queen thought to herself, "Would that I had a child as white as snow, as red as blood, and as black as this ebony window frame."

At last a baby girl was born to her with skin as white as snow, lips red as blood, and hair like the blackest ebony. She named the child Snow White.
But while the child was yet an infant, the queen died.

1: bird, rat, crane, man's face, heads of eagle, dog, pig

In time the king took another wife who was beautiful but terribly proud. High in the castle tower she kept a magic looking glass. She would often stand before the glass and ask . . .

2: squirrel, crow, elephant, candle, face, heads of lion, horse, cat, rabbit

"Mirror, mirror on the wall, who is fairest of us all?"
And the looking glass would reply,
"Thou, O Queen, art the fairest of all."
Then she was content, because the mirror always spoke truthfully.

3: duck, bird, swan, snake, feather, fish, heads of rabbit, goose

As years passed the princess Snow White grew into a beautiful girl. Everyone dwelling in the castle loved her dearly, except the queen.
One day when the queen stood before her looking glass it gave this answer:
"O Queen, the fairest of all is Snow White."

4: flower, hatchet, brontosaurus, duck, fish, heads of goose, ape, eagle

In her jealous hatred she called a huntsman and said, "Take Snow White to the wilderness. Kill her there and bring me her heart as proof that she is dead."

page 5: frog, horse's head, eagle, bird, beaver, face

After the huntsman had led Snow White into the forest he was moved with pity. He released her, saying, "Run quickly, child."
As she disappeared in the shadows, he slew a young fawn and returned to the queen with its heart.
Alone and terrified, Snow White hurried beneath the dark, silent trees. The branches tore her clothing, while small animals darted from her path.

6: flamingo, lizard, dove, heads of alligator, squirrel

7: bat, cardinal, pie, snail, duck, woman, face, hunting bow, heads of mouse, cow, deer, elk

All that day she never rested in her flight. By sunset the exhausted girl came to a clearing in the forest.

There she saw a small cottage. When no one answered her knocking, she opened the door and stepped inside.

8: sea gull, alligator, banana, weasel, heads of rabbit, walrus, wolf

By the dim light she saw a low table with seven little chairs. She took a bit of food from each place and sipped some wine from each mug, so nothing would be missed. Seven small beds were lined up against the wall. Feeling very tired Snow White lay down upon the last one. Closing her eyes, she quickly fell into a deep sleep.

9: shovel, sickle, fork, elf's hat hippopotamus's head, sea horse,

As the moon floated over the surrounding hills, seven dwarves returned from their work in the mines. But after entering the cottage they soon discovered that someone had been eating at their table.

They searched the cottage and finally found Snow White curled up fast asleep. "What a beautiful child," they exclaimed as they gathered round to see. But they were careful not to disturb her.

When Snow White awoke the next morning she was frightened, but the dwarves kindly asked her name and how she had come there.
"I am called Snow White," she replied. She told of her stepmother's plan to kill her, and of her flight through the forest.
"You may dwell here safe from harm," said one, "if you will cook and keep the house clean." Snow White felt safe with the little men and happily agreed.
"We delve in the mountains for copper and gold." But they warned her, "Let no one in while we are gone."

10: lobster, quail, seal, cat, heads of hamster, fox, hawk

11: chicken, snake, spoon, cane, face, horn, fork

12: axe, oar, pear, witch's hat, bird, heads of seal, vulture

That night the queen came again to her looking glass, thinking that Snow White was dead.
"Mirror, mirror on the wall, who is fairest of us all?"
But the glass gave this answer,
"O Queen, your beauty is fair to behold, but Snow White is still fairer a thousandfold."
The huntsman had betrayed her! Now she peered into the glass and saw Snow White safe with the seven dwarves.

The queen pondered what to do while her anger mounted. At last she dressed herself as a peddler woman and journeyed to the mountains to find their cottage.
Knocking at the door, she disguised her voice. "Fine wares to sell," she said.
Snow White looked out and saw only an old peddler.

13: crescent moon, bread, crown, face, shark, heads of parrot, mole

14: heron, butterfly, boot, bluebird, man in the moon, apple

15: parrot, fish, goat, dwarf's face, heads of wolf, dragon

"Laces of every color," said the woman as she held one for the girl to see. Snow White saw no harm and unbolted the door.
"Here's a pretty one," said the woman. "Come and I will lace you with it properly." Then the queen laced her so tightly that Snow White lost her breath and fell senseless.
The queen returned to the castle laughing "Now I am the fairest!".

That evening the seven dwarves found Snow White where she had fallen. Seeing the tight laces that bound her, they quickly cut them away. Soon she began to breathe freely again.
The dwarves now insisted that Snow White should open the door to no one.
Again the queen stood before her looking glass. "Mirror, mirror on the wall, who is the fairest of us all?"
But the glass still replied, "O Queen, Snow White is yet fairest of all."
"Now I will surely put an end to that girl," cried the queen, and she set out for the cottage dressed as a farmer's wife. This time she carried with her a beautiful comb soaked with poison.

"Fine combs for sale," called a voice from outside the cottage.
"I cannot open to anyone," answered Snow White.
Seeing the delicate comb through the window, she finally stepped out for a closer look. But when the comb was placed in her hair, she sank lifeless into the grass.

16: girl's face, kangaroo, heads of bird, puppy, shark, rabbit, pig

17: salamander, mushroom, mouse, chickadee, heads of crow, dog

18: duck, mouse, snake, bird, heads of camel, lion

As they approached the cottage at sunset, the seven dwarves spied Snow White on the ground. Dropping their tools, they removed the comb from her hair, and the girl soon revived. Again they begged her to remain inside.

19: starfish, trout, pointing hand, grasshopper, heads of eagle, horse

That same night the queen strode up to her looking glass.
"Mirror, mirror on the wall, who is the fairest of us all?"
And it gave the answer, "O Queen, Snow White still lives, and her fair beauty surpasses all."
In her fury the queen vowed she would destroy Snow White. Bearing her candle, she climbed to a quiet, lonely tower of the castle.

20: dragonfly, drum, heads of dog, pig, gull, ant

There she lit a fire and gathered all her powers to prepare a fatal poison.
When it was ready she dipped one side of a rosy apple into it. Dressed as a peasant, she again traveled through the wood and knocked at the cottage door. She carried with her a basket of apples with the poisoned one on top.

21: spoon, rake, nail, candle, slice of bread, book

Snow White was busy preparing dinner when a voice called from outside. "Sweet apples for sale."
"The dwarves have forbidden me to open the door," called Snow White from the window.
"As you wish," said the woman, "but I'll give you this one."

The woman bit from the apple and offered the other side to Snow White, saying, "It is perfectly good, as you can see."
The apple looked so delicious that Snow White opened the door and reached out for it. As soon as the apple touched her lips she fell dead to the ground.

22: mop, dagger, bone, crow, teapot, crab

When the seven dwarves returned from the hills, Snow White lay still and not breathing. They lifted her up and searched for anything poisonous, but at last they saw that their beloved child was dead. She looked so fresh and alive they could not bury her in the dark ground. So they made her a coffin out of clear glass.

23: frog, carrot, owl, heads of hippopotamus, cow, deer

They carried her coffin to a high mountain and one of them was always there to watch over her, both day and night.
For a long time Snow White lay unchanged, until one spring a king's son passed through the forest. When he saw the glass coffin on the mountain, he was moved by the girl's beauty.

24: bear, triceratop's head, hamster, seal, Scottie dog, brontosaurus

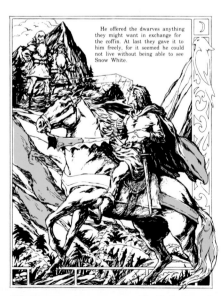

He offered the dwarves anything they might want in exchange for the coffin. At last they gave it to him freely, for it seemed he could not live without being able to see Snow White.

25: tyrannosaurus, scroll, fish, heads of eagle, dog, alligator

As they descended the rocky path, one of the servants stumbled. The poisoned fruit was loosened from Snow White's throat.
"Where am I?" she asked when they had set her down.
"You are here with me," said the prince. "Come to my father's palace to be my wife."
She returned with him happily, and a magnificent wedding was planned.

26: swan, beetle, crane, heads of hawk, pony, ape

The queen was bidden to the celebration, and wearing her finest robes she asked again,
"Mirror, Mirror on the wall, who is fairest of us all?"
And now it gave this answer:
"O Queen, thou art fairest here I hold,
But the new queen is fairer a thousandfold."

She could not resist coming to see the bride. But when the queen saw Snow White beside the prince, she stood motionless with terror. Then red-hot iron shoes were brought for her to dance in until she fell dead.
But Snow White lived joyfully with her prince for the rest of her days.

27: peacock, old man's face, bugle, heads of blue jay, goat, sheep